DISNEY's
Winnie the Pooh
I'm Really Sorry

When you hurt

A friend's feelings,

There's just one thing to do,

Say you're sorry

And mean it.

Then you'll feel good, too.

O n the first warm, sunny day of spring, Pooh decided it was perfect visiting weather. So off he went to Piglet's house. "Hello! Anybody home?" he called, knocking on the door. "I'm home!" cried Piglet.

Piglet joined Pooh outside.

"I'm on my way to visit friends today," said Pooh. "Would you like to come along?"

"I'd love to," replied Piglet, clapping his hands. "Where shall we go first?"

"Perhaps we should visit Rabbit first," said Pooh, thinking about the lovely beehive in Rabbit's tree.

The two friends turned down the path to Rabbit's house. It was then that they heard a loud BOING!

BOING! BOING! BOING!

"Hey there, Buddy Boys!" called Tigger. "Where are you twoses going?"

"To Rabbit's," said Pooh.

"That's a wunnerful idea," declared Tigger. "Can I come, too?"

"Certainly," replied Pooh, pointing toward Rabbit's house.
"Look, there's Rabbit now."

"He's hard at work in his garden," said Piglet.

And Piglet was right, for there stood Rabbit in the middle of his field. And around him were rows and rows of neatly piled dirt all ready for planting carrot seeds and flowers.

"Good thing we came for a visit," said Pooh.
"Now Rabbit can take a rest," added Piglet.
"I'll bounce right over and say 'Hello!'" cried Tigger.

"Hoo-hoo-hoo, Long Ears," Tigger shouted, bouncing higher and higher. But as he bounced, mud flew everywhere. Soon all of Rabbit's neat rows were one big, muddy mess.

"TIGGER!" Rabbit shouted. "Look what you've done!"

"I was just being friendly," announced Tigger. Then he flashed Rabbit a big grin. "Aren't you glad to see me?"

"WHA-WHA-WHA-WHAT?" stammered Rabbit angrily.

Rabbit turned on his heels, went into his house, and slammed the door tight.

"Hey, what happened?" asked Tigger, looking at his friends.

Piglet and Pooh just stared at Tigger sadly.

"Oh, bother. I believe what Rabbit's trying to tell you, Tigger, is that—well—you've made a big mess out here," said Pooh.

"But I was just bouncing. Bouncing is what tiggers do best, you know."

Piglet and Pooh didn't say a word. They just watched as Tigger sputtered and stammered and bounced all around them. Finally he hung his head.

"Aw, this is ridickerous. What should I do?" he asked.

"Let me think, think, think," said Pooh, pacing up and down.
But it was Piglet who had an idea. He told Tigger about it.
"That should do it, Buddy Boy," declared Tigger with a smile.

First, Tigger picked up one of Rabbit's gardening tools.
Then Piglet and Pooh each took one, too. Working together,
they straightened out the rows until everything was as neat as
before. Then they planted carrot seeds.

"Now for the final toucheroo!" said Tigger as the three friends came to the last few rows. Then he bounced and he bounced, and each time he bounced, his tail made a hole in the ground.

And in every hole Tigger made with his bouncy tail, Piglet and Pooh planted colorful flowers.

Tigger stood back and looked at the garden. "Splendiferous," he declared. "Better than before. We can go now. Let's visit Owl!"

As Tigger turned to leave, Piglet rushed up to his friend.
"Tigger, wait!" cried Piglet.
"Now what?" asked Tigger. Piglet had another idea.
"Just tell Rabbit you're sorry," Piglet explained.

"Say I'm sorry? But we fixed the garden," moaned Tigger.
"Besides, Rabbit doesn't want to talk to me."
"But saying you're sorry is the right thing to do," said Pooh.

"But I didn't mean to hurt anything," said Tigger. "I was just being friendly and bouncing. That's what tiggers do."

Pooh and Piglet didn't say a word. Pooh shuffled his feet. Piglet wiggled his ears.

Finally Tigger said, "All right, if it makes ya happy." He knocked on Rabbit's door.

Rabbit opened the door just a tiny little bit. "What do you want?" he asked in a not-too-friendly voice.

"I'm sorry," croaked Tigger.
But Rabbit could tell he didn't mean it.
"Never mind. Just go away," said Rabbit, shutting the door.

Seeing the hurt look on Rabbit's face, Tigger blurted out, "I'm sorry. I didn't mean it. I was just tryin' to be friendly."

Tigger took a deep breath. "I am very, very, very sorry. Really, really, really, Rabbit."

Even Rabbit couldn't help but smile. As he slowly opened the door, Rabbit could see the neatly planted rows of flowers.

"Who did this?" asked a very surprised Rabbit.

"Me, of course," said Tigger proudly. "With a few helpers."

"Thank you for fixing my garden," Rabbit said, smiling. "And for saying you were sorry."

"Anytime," offered Tigger. "Er—Tigger," said Rabbit, "you meant well, but next time do your bouncing somewhere else."

As all the friends laughed, Tigger turned to Pooh and Piglet.
"Gee, saying 'I'm sorry' is kind of special, isn't it?" said Tigger.
"That must be why tiggers say it best!"

A LESSON A DAY
POOH'S WAY

Saying you're sorry

is the right thing to do.